# Terry the Flying Turtle

## ReadZone Books Limited

First published in this edition 2015

© in this edition ReadZone Books Limited 2015
© in text Anna Wilson 2005
© in illustrations Mike Gordon 2005

Anna Wilson has asserted her right under the Copyright Designs and Patents Act 1988 to be identified as the author of this work.

Mike Gordon has asserted his right under the Copyright Designs and Patents Act 1988 to be identified as the illustrator of this work.

Every attempt has been made by the Publisher to secure appropriate permissions for material reproduced in this book. If there has been any oversight we will be happy to rectify the situation in future editions or reprints. Written submissions should be made to the Publisher.

British Library Cataloguing in Publication Data (CIP) is available for this title.

Printed in Malta by Melita Press.

ISBN 978 1 78322 415 9

**Visit our website: www.readzonebooks.com**

# Terry the Flying Turtle

by Anna Wilson

illustrated by Mike Gordon

READZONE

"I'm clever," said Terry the Turtle. Polly the Chimp laughed.

Terry was cross.
"I am clever," said Terry.
"I can fly."

6

Polly laughed and laughed.
"You can't fly!" she said.

Terry was cross.
"I can fly," he said.
"You'll see."

"Will you help me?"
Terry asked the parrot.
"I want to fly."

13

14

The parrot
laughed.
Terry was cross.
"Please will
you help me?"
he asked.

15

"All right," said the parrot.
"Hold this twig and I'll
hold it too."

"Why?" asked Terry.

"Because it will help you fly,"
said the parrot.

The parrot held on.
Terry held on.

21

The parrot flew.
Terry flew!

The animals watched.
"Look at Terry!" they said.
"He looks silly!"

Terry was cross.
"I'm not silly," he shouted.
"You're silly. I'm flying!"

Terry fell down and down.

SPLASH!

28

"You look silly now!" Polly said.

# Did you enjoy this book?

Look out for more *Magpies* titles –
fun stories in 150 words

**The Clumsy Cow** by Julia Moffat and Lisa Williams
ISBN 978 1 78322 157 8

**The Disappearing Cheese** by Paul Harrison and Ruth Rivers
ISBN 978 1 78322 470 8

**Flying South** by Alan Durant and Kath Lucas
ISBN 978 1 78322 410 4

**Fred and Finn** by Madeline Goodey and Mike Gordon
ISBN 978 1 78322 411 1

**Growl!** by Vivian French and Tim Archbold
ISBN 978 1 78322 412 8

**I Wish I Was an Alien** by Vivian French and Lisa Williams
ISBN 978 1 78322 413 5

**Lovely, Lovely Pirate Gold** by Scoular Anderson
ISBN 978 1 78322 206 3

**Pet to School Day** by Hilary Robinson and Tim Archbold
ISBN 978 1 78322 471 5

**Tall Tilly** by Jillian Powell and Tim Archbold
ISBN 978 1 78322 414 2

**Terry the Flying Turtle** by Anna Wilson and Mike Gordon
ISBN 978 1 78322 415 9

**Too Small** by Kay Woodward and Deborah van de Leijgraaf
ISBN 978 1 78322 156 1

**Turn Off the Telly** by Charlie Gardner and Barbara Nascimbeni
ISBN 978 1 78322 158 5